Rita in Wonderworld

Also by Hilda Offen in Happy Cat Books

RITA SERIES

1 Rita the Rescuer

2 Happy Christmas, Rita!

3 Arise, Our Rita!

4 Rita and the Romans

5 Rita at Rushybrook Farm

6 Roll Up! Roll Up! It's Rita

7 Rita and the Flying Saucer

8 Rita in Wonderworld

PICTURE BOOKS

Elephant Pie

Good Girl, Gracie Growler!

Umbrella Weather

Rita in Wonderworld

Hilda Offen

Happy Cat Books

For Billy

HAPPY CAT BOOKS

Published by Happy Cat Books Ltd.
Bradfield, Essex CO11 2UT, UK

This edition first published 2003
1 3 5 7 9 10 8 6 4 2

A CIP catalogue record for this book is available from the British Library

ISBN 1 903285 63 1

Printed in China by Midas Printing Limited.

"Look! There it is! There's Wonderworld!" cried Eddie.

"I can hardly wait!" said Jim. "I'm going into the Ghost Grotto."

"Me too!" said Eddie. "I've heard it's really scary."

"And I'm going on the Dino-Coaster," said Julie.

"What about you, Rita?" asked Uncle Bill.

"Huh! Rita's too young for the rides!" snorted Eddie. "She'd be scared."

Wonderworld was packed.

"Phew! That was quite a drive!" said Uncle Bill, flopping down in the picnic area. "I need a nap."

"You can all go off on your own," said Auntie Sal. "But take care of Rita."

"Follow us, Rita!" said Julie. "We know just the place for you."

They stopped in front of a notice which said "Chicks' Nest Play Area".

"Are you lost?" asked a lady in a chicken outfit. She grasped Rita's hand. "Come inside! I have a special little tricycle you can play on."

Eddie, Julie and Jim ran away.

"We'll soon find your family," said the Chicken Lady. "Now – what's your name?"

Huh! thought Rita. I'm not going to spend the day playing on a tricycle.

She jumped into the Ball Pool and burrowed down till she was out of

sight. Then she took her Rescuer's outfit from her rucksack and started to change.

"My goodness! What was that?" gasped the Chicken Lady. It was Rita, shooting past her in a blaze of light!

"Now for some rescues," said Rita.

She didn't have to look far. Little Kevin Tucker was crying his eyes out. He couldn't steer his Bumper Bug and everyone kept thudding into him.

Rita landed in the seat next to him.

"Hold tight!" she said and started to whizz Kevin round like a racing driver. They didn't hit a single Bug.

"Can we have another go?" asked Kevin as the ride came to an end.

But Rita was off again. She had heard a scream.

Victor the Viking had lost his balance! Rita caught him just before he hit the ground and set him back on his tightrope.

"It's best to try again as soon as possible," she said.

"I'll just practise quietly at the side," said Victor. "Can you show us how it should be done, Rescuer?"

So Rita rode Victor's unicycle backwards and forwards across the rope, juggled with six balls and cooked a pancake – all at the same time!

"Bravo!" cried the spectators. But Rita was off. Her sharp ears had caught the sound of a wail.

"I recognize that voice!" said Rita

Julie was standing by the Ghost Grotto.

"Eddie and Jim went in!" she cried. "But they haven't come out. Look – their boat's empty!"

"I'll find them!" said Rita.

"But it's dark in there!" quavered Julie. "It's full of ghosts and skeletons! And bats and rats! And giant spiders!"

"They don't scare me," said Rita. "Besides, I can see in the dark."

Inside the grotto, Eddie and Jim were caught in a huge spider's web. They were shaking like jellies.

"What ever happened to you?" asked Rita.

"We were trying to catch a bat," said Jim. "But we leaned too far."

Rita untangled them and flew them back to the exit.

"Hooray for the Rescuer!" cried Julie.

"I have to go!" said Rita. "I'm needed at the waterchute!"

Jenny Jones had shot from her spinning teacup! She whirled through the air and disappeared beneath the foam.

Rita did a running dive.

"Don't panic!" she said.

She held Jenny's head above water and guided her down to the bottom of the waterchute where her parents were waiting.

"Make sure she does up her safety belt next time," said Rita. "Uh-oh – here we go again!"

There was trouble at the ticket office!

"Stop, thief!" yelled Mr Wonder.

A gorilla had grabbed the takings and was running off through the crowd.

"Not so fast!" said Rita and she launched herself into a flying rugby tackle. The gorilla crashed to the ground.

"This is not a gorilla at all!" said Rita. She whipped off a rubber mask. "It's Larry Lightfingers, the well-known bank robber!"

Mr Wonder came puffing up with a policeman, but there was no time for thank-yous. Something awful was happening above their heads. The Dino-Coaster was out of control and travelling at the speed of light!

"Help!" screamed Julie. "I feel sick!"

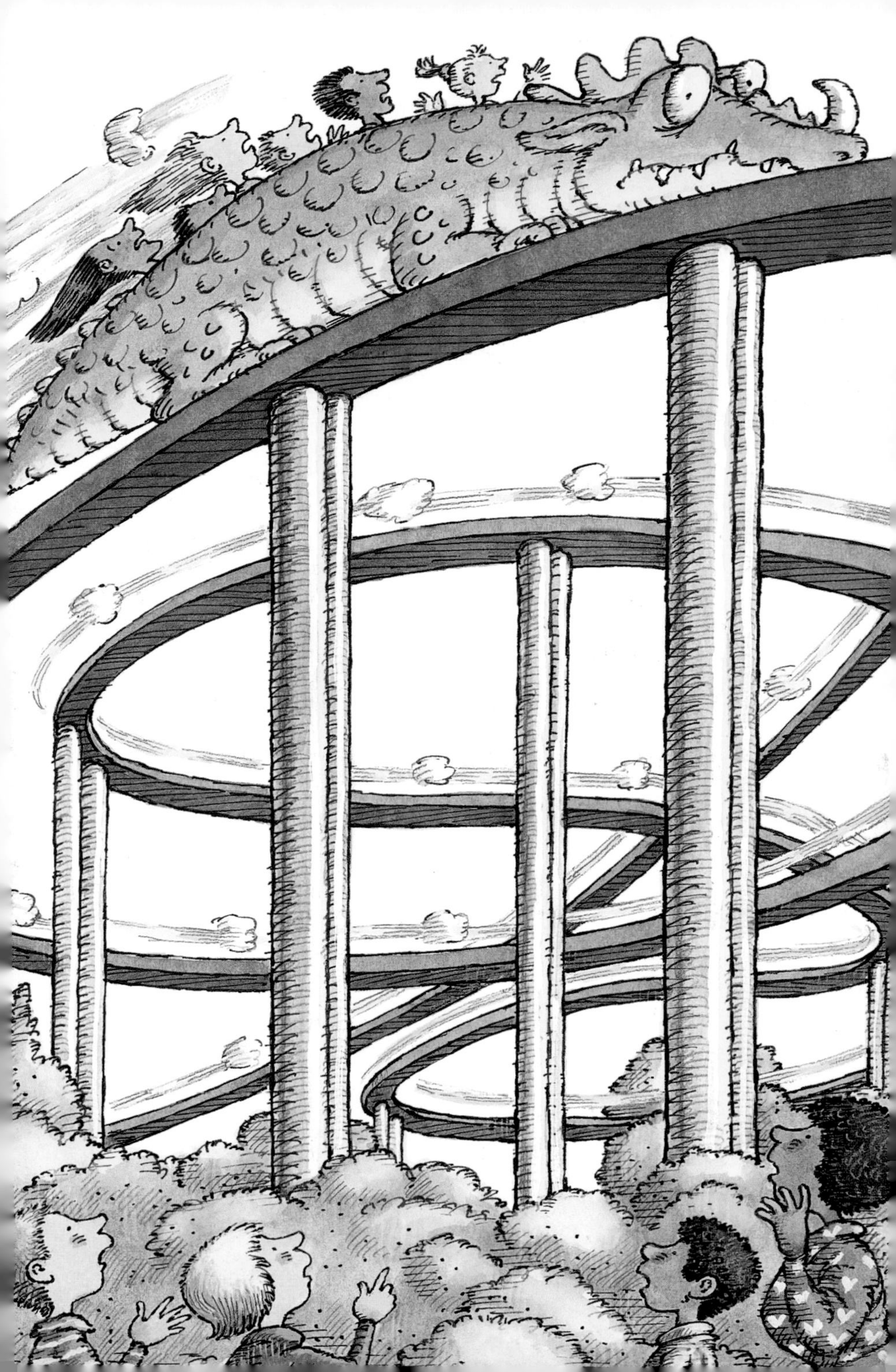

Rita zoomed upwards and caught the Dino-Coaster by the tail. She hung on as hard as she could and everything ground to a halt.

"Three cheers for the Rescuer!" cried Mr Wonder as Rita pushed the Dino-Coaster safely back to the ground.

"You've just got to give me your autograph!" said Julie as she clambered down.

"Sorry!" said Rita. "Things to do!"

She could hear the lost children screaming in the Chicks' Nest.

"The loudspeaker's broken!" gasped the Chicken Lady.

"Leave it to me!" said Rita and she soared up into the sky.

"SILENCE!" she roared.

The Big Wheel stopped turning. The Pirate Ship stopped swinging. Everything went quiet.

"WOULD ANYONE WHO HAS LOST A CHILD COME TO THE CHICKS' NEST – AT ONCE!" roared Rita.

Soon all the lost children had been claimed by their parents.

"Rescuer – please accept this Golden Ticket," said Mr Wonder. "It gives you free entry to Wonderworld for life."

"Oh, thank you!" said Rita. "Time I was off, though."

She dived into the Ball Pool.

She had seen Eddie, Julie and Jim coming to collect her.

In no time at all she had changed back into little Rita Potter.

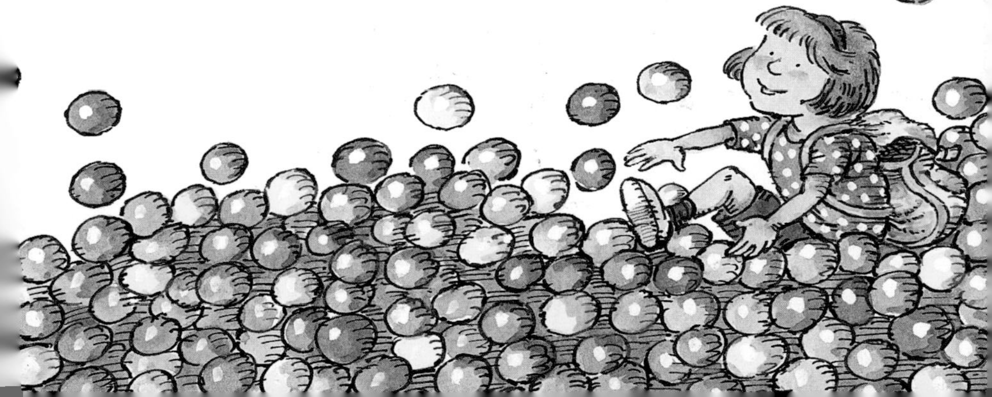

"So, Rita!" giggled Eddie on the way home. "How was the Chicks' Nest?"

"You missed the Rescuer again!" said Jim. "She got us out of the Ghost Grotto."

"And she saved me on the Dino-Coaster!" cried Julie. "She was brilliant!"

Rita smiled to herself and thought about her Golden Ticket.

"Oh well!" she said. "Better luck next time!"

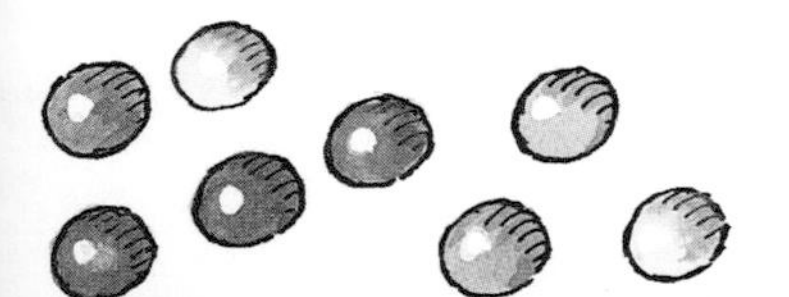

Other Rita titles available in Happy Cat Paperbacks

Rita the Rescuer

When you are the youngest in the family, you can sometimes get left out of the fun. Then one day Rita Potter is sent a magical Rescuer's outfit which gives her amazing powers… Three cheers for Rita!

Arise, Our Rita!

Rita may be the youngest of the Potter family, but she also is the fabulous Rescuer! And teaching archery to Robin Hood, taming dragons and giants, is all in a day's work for our pint-sized superhero.

Rita and the Romans

Left behind in the Potter family's Wendy-house it is lucky Rita has her Rescuer's outfit to hand. In no time at all she rescuing toddlers, saving gladiators and even building Adrian's Wall!

Roll Up! Roll Up! It's Rita

Rita's family thinks she is too small to dress up for the school fair. But Rita has her own special Rescuer's costume and in the blink of an eye she is saving a hot-air balloon, rounding up sheep and winning the tug-of-war single-handed!